A GIRL'S BILL OF RIGHTS

by AMY B. MUCHA

ILLUSTRATED by ADDY RIVERA SONDA

beaming books
MINNEAPOLIS

27 26 25 24 23 22 21   1 2 3 4 5 6 7 8

Hardcover ISBN: 978-1-5064-6452-7
Ebook ISBN: 978-1-5064-6664-4

Written by Amy B. Mucha
Illustrated by Addy Rivera Sonda

Library of Congress Cataloging-in-Publication Data

Names: Mucha, Amy B., author. | Sonda, Addy Rivera, illustrator.
Title: A girl's bill of rights / by Amy B. Mucha ; illustrated by Addy
   Rivera Sonda.
Description: Minneapolis, MN : Beaming Books, 2021. | Audience: Ages 5-8. |
   Summary: "In a world where little girls must learn to stand tall, A
   Girl's Bill of Rights boldly declares the rights of every woman and
   girl: power, confidence, freedom, and consent"-- Provided by publisher.
Identifiers: LCCN 2019056261 (print) | LCCN 2019056262 (ebook) | ISBN
   9781506464527 (hardcover) | ISBN 9781506466644 (ebook)
Subjects: CYAC: Women's rights--Fiction. | Self-acceptance--Fiction.
Classification: LCC PZ7.1.M74 Gi 2021 (print) | LCC PZ7.1.M74 (ebook) |
   DDC [E]--dc23
LC record available at https://lccn.loc.gov/2019056261
LC ebook record available at https://lccn.loc.gov/2019056262

VN0004589; 9781506464527; NOV2020

Beaming Books
510 Marquette Avenue
Minneapolis, MN 55402
Beamingbooks.com

I have the right to like what I like
and love what I love.

I have the right to look how I look and wear what I wear

and do whatever I want with my hair.

I have the right to think for myself and choose for myself, to say "Yes!" if I want something...

and "No" if I don't,

and the right to change my mind.

I have the right to speak my truth,
even if someone doesn't want to hear it.

I have the right to feel what I feel, every moment,
even if it makes someone uncomfortable.

I have the right to laugh

and the right to cry.

I have the right to feel scared

and the right to get mad.

I have the right to make mistakes, even big ones,

and the right to forgive myself.

I have the right to choose my friends,

and the right to hug
or high five or smile,

or not to smile.

If someone is hurting or disrespecting me,

I have the right to say "STOP!"
and even the right to SCREAM it!

Because it is NOT OK
to hurt me.
Or anyone.
Not ever.

I have the right to be bold and mighty and LOUD!

And the right to
be silly and awkward

and PROUD!

I have the right to decide who I'll be,

for now, for tomorrow, and forever.

Because most of all, no matter what,

I absolutely always

have the right to be ME.

We all do!

 **AMY B. MUCHA** grew up in New York and New Jersey and now lives in Chapel Hill, North Carolina, with her husband, two children, two spoiled dogs, four superior cats, and hundreds of books. When she isn't writing, she can be found reading, daydreaming, sipping tea, and eating chocolate medicinally. Amy is passionate about empowering girls and women everywhere to love themselves, embrace and support all the girls in their lives, and speak loud for what's right.

 **ADDY RIVERA SONDA** is a Mexican illustrator, who loves color and nature. When she is not drawing, she devotes a great part of her time to learning and exploring ways in which we could live kinder and more sustainable lives.

Her biggest inspiration for drawing is that she knows that stories and art can shape the way people understand themselves and perceive others, building empathy and ultimately a happier, more inclusive world.